I Can Read...
Hansel and Gretel

Once upon a time, there were two
children called Hansel and Gretel.
Hansel and Gretel lived with their
father and stepmother.
Their father was a woodcutter.
He was kind.
Their stepmother was not kind at all.

Hansel and Gretel lived with their
father and stepmother.

They were very poor.
There was no food to eat.
One day, Hansel heard his stepmother
talking to his father.
"The children eat too much," said the
stepmother. "Take them into the woods
and leave them there. Then I can have
all the food."
Hansel thought of a plan. Hansel filled
his pockets with white stones.

Hansel filled his pockets with white stones.

The next day, all the family went into the woods. As they walked, Hansel secretly dropped the white stones one at a time.

The father made a fire to keep them warm. Hansel and Gretel fell asleep by the fire.

When they woke up, it was dark.

They were all alone.

Hansel and Gretel fell asleep by the fire.

Hansel and Gretel followed the stones
back to their house.
Their stepmother was angry.
She took them back into the woods.
Hansel had no more stones, so he
dropped breadcrumbs instead.
Hansel and Gretel fell asleep again.

Hansel and Gretel followed the stones back to their house.

When they woke up, they were all alone.
The birds had eaten all the breadcrumbs.
They could not find the way home.
Hansel and Gretel found a cottage made
out of gingerbread and sweets.

Hansel and Gretel found a cottage
made out of gingerbread and sweets.

The house belonged to a wicked witch.
She pretended to be kind at first.
She gave Hansel and Gretel lovely food
to eat. But then she locked Hansel
in a cage.
The witch made Gretel do all the work.

The house belonged to
a wicked witch.

The witch gave Hansel lots of food.
"I will eat you when you are nice and
fat," she said.
Every day, the witch felt Hansel's finger.
But she could not see very well.
Hansel put a twig in her hand instead
of his finger.
The witch thought Hansel was skinny.

The witch gave Hansel lots of food.

Soon the witch got tired of waiting.
"You are not nice and fat but I will eat
you anyway," said the witch.
The witch told Gretel to make the
oven hot.

The witch told Gretel to make
the oven hot.

Gretel lit the fire.

The witch let Hansel out of the cage.

Hansel and Gretel pushed the witch into the cage.

They locked the door.

The witch could not hurt anyone ever again.

The witch let Hansel out of the cage.

Hansel and Gretel ran back to their house.
Their father was very happy to see them.
Their stepmother was never seen again.